THE BULLY CAT

BY NADIA SAHARI

TO AUSTIN,
Inspiration!

Illustrated by

Olga Rudnitsky

ONE DAY

Daddy Scott, Mommy Agnes and their two children, Maia and Raiden moved into their new house along with their two pet cats Crimson and Clover.

They were so excited.

They opened the door and ran in almost knocking each other down.

Crimson and Clover ran the fastest.

The house was beautiful.

It was way bigger than the house they had before.

"WOW!!! WHAT A BIG HOUSE!"

exclaimed Maia and Raiden together.

The children quickly claimed their bedrooms
and began unpacking their clothes and toys,

but Raiden's mind was on Daddy Scott's iPad.

Raiden was three years old and always had a big smile on his face—well, most of the time. Sometimes he was a clown.
HE MADE GRANDPA LAUGH OUT LOUD.
He always wanted Grandpa to lift him up high in the air.
He laughed so hard he almost fell down.
Grandpa was always careful. He didn't want to hurt Raiden.
It was so much fun when Grandpa and Nana came over.

Uncle Ken would come over, too!
He brought his dog Lucy with him.

Crimson and Clover did not like that at all.

They would hide somewhere in the house and no one could find them until late at night.

Uncle Ken could lift Raiden way up to the ceiling because he was OVER SIX FEET TALL.

Raiden loved playing with the iPad more than his toys.

He couldn't wait to sit on the sofa with it.

He PLAYED GAMES FOR HOURS.

He was very fast and he won lots of times.

When Nana, Grandpa and Uncle Ken came over,
he would show them how to play the games.
THEY WERE SO PROUD OF HIM.

Maia was six years old. She was a ballerina
and she danced on her tippy toes.
She wore a PINK tutu
and PINK ballerina slippers and PINK tights.

Maia loved to **PLAY THE PIANO**, too, and she was very good. She played the piano and sang for Nana, Grandpa and Uncle Ken when they came over to visit.

They never missed her piano recitals. They sat and listened and always clapped when Maia was finished. Nana took lots of pictures. They were **SO PROUD OF HER.**

Maia had a big smile on her face all the time, too. Well, sometimes she did frown. Nana, Grandpa and Uncle Ken laughed when she frowned. That made Maia **LAUGH** too!

When Mommy Agnes and Daddy Scott **FINISHED UNPACKING**, they sat down to rest for a while with a glass of water.

Mommy Agnes was looking at their big backyard with all the lovely oak trees when all of a sudden she noticed **SOMETHING MOVE.**

She called out to Daddy Scott,
"**HURRY!** Come and see what I see!"

There they were—CATS! Daddy Scott counted them and there were **TEN STRAY CATS!**

"**OH MY!** What should we do?" exclaimed Mommy Agnes. "Let's trap them **ONE AT A TIME** before they have more kittens," said Daddy Scott. "They can stay here as long as they wish. We will feed them every day."

Maia and Raiden ran down the stairs yelling YAY!
They were so thrilled to see all the cats outside.
Crimson and Clover saw the ten cats outside too and began
meowing and snarling. Maia and Raiden laughed and said,
"It's okay Crimson and Clover. They won't Come inside.
They won't bother you."

So Mommy Agnes and Daddy Scott
trapped the stray cats one at
a time and took them all to the
vet to be spayed or neutered so
they wouldn't make baby cats.
Otherwise, if they didn't do
something quickly there might be
hundreds of homeless cats to feed.

The vet said, "I wish there were
MORE PEOPLE LIKE YOU
who were responsible and cared
for the animals. It is up to us
to protect them." "Yes, I agree,"
said Daddy Scott. "It is a smart
thing to help the animals."

They returned home and released all the cats into the backyard. They fed all the cats and gave them fresh water to drink. All the cats were hungry after visiting the vet. Maia and Raiden were excited to have **TEN NEW PETS!**

Crimson and Clover were not too sure what was going on with the cats outside, but they were loved and cared for. They had no worries. After all, they were inside.

Maia and Raiden jumped up and down, "Can we name all the cats outside? Please, Mommy and Daddy?"

"Sure, go ahead. Raiden, you name five cats and Maia, you name the other five cats. Maia, you go first," said Mommy Agnes.

Maia named them one at a time. "The momma cat is CRAYOLA because she is painted black, orange, white and gray. She is so beautiful. Her nose is black and her eyes light brown," she said. "I like that," said Mommy Agnes.

"The daddy cat . . . hmmmmmm. I will name him BIG DADDY because he is the biggest of all. He's black with yellow eyes," continued Maia. "Okay, that's two, Maia, three more to go," said Mommy Agnes.

"I think that kitten's name should be PATCHES," said Maia pointing to a calico. "She's got all the colors like the mommy cat; orange, black, gray and white."

"OOOH! That one looks like a baby lion. Look, Mommy, he has a mane like a lion. Can I call him BRUISER?" "Of course," replied Mommy Agnes, "he is beautiful!"

"And look at that one," said Maia, "he is so sweet, like sugar. SUGAR, that's his name. He always wants me to touch him and hold him. He is gentle and makes me laugh. Mommy, his colors are the same as Patches, but his fur is fluffy and soft," giggled Maia. "Good job, Maia!" Mommy Agnes was very happy with the names Maia had chosen.

"Okay, your turn, Raiden." Daddy Scott was happy to help Raiden. "Daddy, I want that one to be called SPOOKY because she's scared. She always runs away from me. And Daddy, can I name that one CRAYON?" "Sure," replied Daddy Scott. "What about the light gray and white kitten over there? She looks so pretty. Her eyes are big and she is soft and gentle, too!" "How about we name her CAMEO?" asked Raiden. "Oh, that's a good name," said Daddy Scott, "she looks just like a cameo."

"Look at that black cat," Daddy. "He is shiny black and his eyes are like gold coins. Daddy, let's call him **BLACKIE**!" Raiden was so excited. "And that one must be Bruiser's sister," said Raiden, "I'll call her GINGER." "Good job, Raiden!" said Daddy Scott.

ALL THE CATS WERE BEAUTIFUL AND UNIQUE, JUST LIKE KIDS.

All kids are unique and special. All ten cats had a name and now everyone was happy.

"How about we have dinner now that all the cats have names," Mommy Agnes said. "Everyone should be hungry by now." YAY!!! Maia and Raiden were happy to eat. It had been a long day. YUMMY!!! They all sat at the table to enjoy dinner together.

The next day everyone was happy and rested.
All the cats were fed and happy, too! Well, almost.

Daddy Scott said, "Oh! Oh! Who's that?" Everyone looked outside and saw a mean-looking cat. He was black as black can be and white as white can be. His face looked mean and rough. He scared all the other cats away, and he ate up all the food and didn't leave anything for the other cats.

"Where did he come from?" asked Maia. "I have no idea," said Daddy Scott, "but he is trouble. He is a BULLY CAT!" Maia and Raiden looked at each other with their eyes as big as pies! "BULLY CAT!!!" they repeated. "What are we going to do?" asked Mommy Agnes.

The family waited to see what the BULLY CAT would do before they decided what to do. When dinner time came, they watched and they waited.

"HERE HE COMES!"

everyone yelled.

"He walks like he is a star," Mommy Agnes said laughing. "Let's call him STAR," and everyone laughed.

Star was strutting toward the food on the patio where all the other cats were eating peacefully. They took one look at him and ran away—except for Sugar.

All of a sudden Star walked up face to face with Sugar. Sugar was eating and minding his own business, but Star wanted his food, no matter if the rest of the bowls had food too! He wanted Sugar's bowl.

Sugar and Star stood staring at each other.

It was a **FACE OFF!** Sugar slowly sauntered away,
but his eyes never left Star's eyes.
When Sugar had a chance, he ran away as fast as could.

"Boy! What can we do? We can't let this bully scare our cats every day," Daddy Scott said nervously.

Just then everyone heard loud meows: MEOW!!!!! MEOW!!!! MEOW!!!! Together they opened the door and ran outside to see what was wrong.

Star was beating up Bruiser, the nicest cat of them all. Fur was flying everywhere in the air, but as soon as Star saw Maia and Raiden he ran away so fast they couldn't see him anymore.

Bruiser was whipped! Poor Bruiser. "Sorry Bruiser, we won't let Star hurt you anymore.

DADDY! MOMMY! Star beat up Bruiser and scared everybody away! He's a BULLY CAT for sure," cried Maia.

"All right! That's it!" Daddy Scott said calmly. Star is going to be someone's barn cat. We have to trap him and send him away. I will call the Mountainside Animal League and they can help us find him a new home. Mommy Agnes grabbed her cell phone and called the Animal League right away. It was the hardest thing to do. The whole family loved animals.

The next morning the sun was shining and Daddy Scott set the trap with a loving heart. Daddy Scott placed a dish of tuna in the trap and waited for Star to go in after it.

It didn't take long. Star came strolling by and sniffing in the air. He smelled the tuna right away.

He walked right into the trap
and **BOOM! SLAM! BANG!**

The sound scared everybody! Star jumped as high as
he could in the trap, but it was done. He was trapped.
He was so scared now. Raiden asked Daddy Scott
why Star was so scared and not brave.

"That's how bullies are, Raiden, they pick
on someone who is smaller and nicer than
them. Bullies are afraid to pick on anyone
bigger or smarter than they are. The
truth is, Raiden, the bully does not feel
good about himself. He knows he is weak;
that's why he picks on others. But if you
are smart and a good person, there is no
need to prove anything to anyone."
Daddy Scott placed Star inside the
truck and drove away to drop him off at
the Animal League.

Everyone felt really bad to send Star
away. He was special, too. They were all
sad. But they had to do it. Star just was
not nice to the other cats. So he had
to go away and live somewhere
in a barn all alone.

With Star gone, the other cats were happy and at peace. They were all having their dinner. NO BULLY HERE! It was nice to see, the way it should be. The family looked at each other and wondered if someday Star would come back and treat everybody the way they should be treated and be a nice cat.

Daddy Scott said, "Well, maybe one day Star will learn his lesson and make the choice to be a nicer cat. Maybe he will treat the other cats kinder and get along with them, and he will definitely miss the food here at our house. We were good to him. He had it made. Now, the poor thing will be eating mice and bugs if he can find them. That's what barn cats eat. Maia and Raiden looked at each other with wide eyes. They both exclaimed, "YUCK! MICE AND BUGS!!!" And then they giggled.

Raiden asked Daddy Scott a question that bothered him all day long. "Daddy, if I have a fight with a boy in school, would you send me off to a barn?" "NO WAY!" Daddy Scott laughed. "But don't you ever pick a fight with anyone, not in school or out of school. You should learn to get along with all the kids and help them whenever they need help.

If someone bullies you like Star bullied the cats, tell me or Mommy. We will take care of you and keep you safe. Never keep it a secret. You must always tell us or we will never know or be able to help you. That goes for you too, Maia. "Okay, Daddy," they both happily replied and smiled at each other.

"It's always best to be nice and to help each other. The world would be a better place if everyone just loved each other and accepted each other," said Daddy Scott.

"Yeah, Raiden," Maia quickly responded to what her daddy said. "Don't pull my hair anymore or Daddy will send you away." "No, he won't," said Raiden, not really sure what Daddy Scott would do. Daddy Scott just looked at both of them and smiled.

"Raiden, tell your sister you're sorry for pulling her hair and you will never do it again!"

Raiden looked Maia right in the face, "I'm sorry, Maia."

"That's okay, Raiden. But don't ever do it again—you promise?" "I promise," replied Raiden.

They hugged each other and off they went to play with their toys. "Maia, I love you," said Raiden. "I love you too, Raiden," said Maia.

Mommy Agnes and Daddy Scott hugged each other and said "I LOVE YOU" to each other. After all, that's how Maia and Raiden learned to love each other.

That's how they learned to be nice to other kids and nice to all the animals. LOVE starts at home and then it goes real far away outside to everyone else.

Inquiries should be addressed to:

Cedar Leaf Press

17503 La Cantera Parkway

Suite 104-240

San Antonio, TX 78257

www.cedarleafpress.com

Library of Congress Cataloging-in-Publication Data

Sahari, Nadia [date]

The Bully Cat

www.thebullycat.com

ISBN 978-0-9820413-9-0 (paper)

Library of Congress Control Number: 2011919591

1. Sahari, Nadia [date] 2. Children's Literature

3. Children Ages 4-8

Printed in the United States of America

Printed on acid-free paper

This book is CPSIA Compliant

CPSIA information can be obtained
at www.ICGtesting.com
Printed in the USA
LVIC041031171211
259753LV00004B